An Alien Dies

Look for other **ANIMORPHS**
titles by K.A. Applegate:

An Alien Dies

the andalite chronicles

K.A. Applegate

AN
APPLE
PAPERBACK

SCHOLASTIC INC.
New York Toronto London Auckland Sydney

ISBN 0-590-10881-6

12 11 10 9 8 7 6 5 4 3 2 1   7 8 9/9 0 1 2/0

Printed in the U.S.A.   40

First Scholastic printing, November 1997

For Michael and Jake

Prologue

My name is Elfangor.

I am an Andalite prince. And I am about to die.

My fighter is damaged. I have crash-landed on the surface of the planet called Earth. I believe that my great Dome ship has been destroyed. I fear that my little brother Aximili is already dead.

We did not expect the Yeerks to be here in such force. We made a mistake. We underestimated the Yeerks. Not for the first time. We would have defeated their Pool ship and its fighters. But there was a Blade ship in orbit as well.

The Blade ship of Visser Three.

Two Yeerk Bug fighters are landing on either side of me now. The abomination Visser Three is here as well. I can feel him. I can sense his evil.

I cannot defeat the visser in one-on-one combat. I am weak from my injuries. Too weak to morph. Too weak to fight.

This is my *hirac delest* — my final statement. I have formed the mental link to the thought-speak transponder in my fighter's computer. I will record my memories before the Yeerks annihilate all trace of me.

If this message someday reaches the Andalite world, I want the truth to be known. I am called a great warrior. A hero. But there is a great deal that no Andalite knows about me. I have not lied, but I have kept the truth a secret.

This is not my first visit to Earth. I spent many years on Earth . . . and yet, no time at all.

I landed here now in this construction site be-cause I was looking for a great weapon: the Time Matrix. The existence of this weapon is also a secret.

So many secrets in my life . . . mistakes. Things I should have done. All the strands of my strange life seem to be coming together. It all seems inevitable now. Of course my death would come on Earth. Of course my child would be here. Of course it would be Visser Three who would take my life.

I am too weak to locate the Time ship now. I will die here. But I have left a legacy. Visser Three thinks he has won our long, private war. But I've left a little surprise behind.

I have given the morphing power to five human youths.

I know that in doing this I have broken Andalite law. I know that this action will be condemned by all my people. But the Yeerks are here on Earth. Visser Three is here. The humans must be given a chance to resist. The human race cannot fall to the Yeerks the way the Hork-Bajir race did.

I have given the morphing power to five young humans. Children, really. But sometimes children can accomplish amazing things.

I have no choice but to hope. Because it was I who created Visser Three. I who caused the abomination. I cannot go peacefully to my death, knowing that I created the creature who will enslave the human race.

I came to this place, this empty construction site, looking for the weapon I know is hidden here. But there is no time now. No time . . .

The Visser is here. He is laughing at my weakness. He is savoring his victory over me.

This is the *hirac delest* of Elfangor-Sirinial-Shamtul, Andalite prince. I open my mind in the ritual of death. I open my mind and let all my memories — all my secrets — go to be recorded by the computer.

This is not just a message to my own people. I hope that someday humans will read it as well. Because humans are also my people. Loren . . . and the boy I have just met, but not for the first time. . . .

An Alien Dies

chapter 1

Air!

My lungs burned. My hearts pounded desperately. My mind was shutting down from lack of oxygen. As I faded out, a deadly weariness took the place of terror.

The ship's artificial gravity was gone. I floated, weightless, as the floor and walls and ceiling all spun wildly around me.

Why should I care? Why should I resist? Why not just let it all end, here, now, as the *Jahar* fell into the monstrous black hole?

My life was a disaster. I had failed in so many ways. . . . Failed to save Arbron from being trapped forever in Taxxon morph. Failed to stop the Yeerk called Visser Thirty-two from stealing the body of my prince, Alloran-Semitur-Corrass. Failed to defeat the surprise attack of the living asteroids. Failed even to protect the two humans I was supposed to take care of.

And worst of all, I had failed to deliver the Time Matrix to my people. The Time Matrix: power beyond imagination.

Airless! My head swam with disconnected thoughts and images. Airless! In a ship that spun powerless, dead, through space.

Through the still-clear window I saw the huge swirl of dust and debris that marked the approaches to the black hole. But at the center of that swirl, nothing the eye could see. It was a collapsed star so dense that its gravity trapped light itself.

Yes, Elfangor, my dying mind said, let it end.

I saw the abomination, Visser Thirty-two, the only Andalite-Controller in the galaxy. The only Yeerk ever to gain control of an Andalite body. He was swooning from the lack of oxygen. He was slammed by the spinning floor and knocked, weightless, into the ceiling, four legs flailing, arms and tail all tangled around.

I held on to a protrusion in the control panel. But as the ship twirled, with all gravity gone, I felt something large and soft bump into me.

It was Loren. The female human. Unconscious. Never to be conscious again, if I didn't reach the emergency air supply and use the manual release.

And then it came to me, in a moment of clarity: I had no choice. When Arbron had been in utter despair and had wanted to die, I stopped him. Because without life there is no despair, but without life there can also never be hope.

I had no right to erase Loren's hope, no matter how bad I felt.

I searched my crazy, swirling, nightmare world with all my eyes and found the panel I was searching for. I focused on it with my stalk eyes, striving blearily to keep them focused.

But it was so hard. So hard to know up from down, left from right, with all the world spinning, and my own poor oxygen-deprived brain all but extinguished.

Had to reach that panel.

I would have one chance. One only. Too far gone to try a second time.

I aimed and kicked and flew weightless across the cabin. Missed! I grabbed. Missed! I floated helplessly away.

Suddenly, a hand reached up and shoved me back toward the panel. A *human* hand! Impossible! Loren had regained consciousness. In a near vacuum. Without air. With temperatures already dropping toward absolute zero!

She had regained consciousness. And seen what I was trying to do. She had propelled me back toward the panel. This time I reached and grabbed. I ripped the panel open, and turned the stiff mechanical release knob.

You cannot see air, of course. You don't really feel it on your skin, most of the time. But when it is gone, you notice it.

My lungs sucked and drew nothing in. Nothing!

My lungs gasped again, and this time, I sensed just the faintest wisp of something.

I sucked again and <aaaahhh!> A sharp pain as my collapsed lungs filled with air.

Air! I drew deep breath after deep breath, each breath hurting, but hurting less than the one before. It was not a pain I minded.

I clung to the panel with my left hand, my hooves floating free, my tail drifting behind me. And for a while I just breathed, and thanked the entire universe for letting me feel air in my lungs again.

<Are you all right?> I asked Loren.

She smiled a human smile, the characteristic upturning of the corners of her mouth. It was a weak, shaky smile. But I was glad to see it.

"I thought we were done for," she said.

<Done for? Oh. Dead. Yes, we almost were. But you humans don't give up easily, do you?>

"Neither do you Andalites," she said. "Now what?"

I surveyed the situation. The visser appeared to be just regaining consciousness. The other human, Chapman, was still unconscious, drifting lazily against the far wall like a rag doll.

<Well, we have air, but no power. The living asteroids drained the ship of power. We are falling toward a black hole.>

"Oh. That's not good," she said.

<If we fall into the black hole it will crush us down to the size of a carbon atom. The ship, all of us, crushed to the size of a single atom.>

"Yeah, we learned about black holes in school."

I was surprised that humans knew about such things.

<There is only one way out, Andalite.>

Visser Thirty-two. The very sound of his thought-speak voice in my head filled me with rage. He sounded exactly like Alloran. But I knew that Alloran's mind was a prisoner in his own head now. He could watch, listen, feel, but not control. The Yeerk in his brain controlled him now. The Yeerk moved his arms and legs and tail. The Yeerk decided when each breath would be drawn. The Yeerk aimed his eyes and formed his thought-speech.

I turned myself to face him. I had no idea which of us would win a tail fight. He had Alloran's experience. But I had seen that I was faster than Alloran.

<Don't be a fool, Elfangor,> the visser sneered. <What will be gained by you and me slashing each other up with these excellent Andalite tails?>

<You have a better idea?> I asked. <Because I can think of a lot of good reasons to go tail-to-tail with you.>

The visser laughed. <You blame me for all your own failings? I'm not the one who left his friend back on the Taxxon world, trapped in that vile worm's body. I'm not the one who disobeyed his prince's orders and let ten thousand Yeerks escape. A bit of disobedience that helped cause poor old Alloran's downfall.>

I wanted to shrug off his words. But there was truth in them. And it is hard to ignore the truth. And pointless, as well.

<You have something to say, Yeerk?>

<Yes. We are falling toward a black hole in a dead ship. But we have a way out. The Time Matrix.>

I stared at him with my main eyes. But my stalk eyes saw Loren look at me with fresh hope.

<In case you haven't noticed, Visser, the Time Matrix is strapped to the outside of the ship. The *outside*. In fact, it's probably drifting free. It was held in place with energy ropes. Those are gone.>

<Gravity,> the Yeerk said. <There should be just enough attraction between the ship and the Time Matrix to keep it close.>

I did the familiar calculations in my head. He was right. The Time Matrix was probably still just outside the ship.

<How do you propose getting to it?> I asked.

<We would have to work together, Andalite. And quickly.>

chapter 2

<Work together?>

<One of us will have to be reeled outside. On a rope or cable. Someone will have to hold that rope. And someone else will have to be on the end of that rope.>

<And do what? Pull the Time Matrix in through the hatch? That will mean losing all our air again. We don't have force fields anymore.>

<Yes. It will be do-or-die,> the visser said. <We can use the air hoods for an emergency five minutes.>

I stared blankly at him. <What air hoods?>

<You forget I control Alloran. And this was his ship. I know all the ship's secrets. There is a small supply of emergency hoods. Alloran kept them for just such an occasion.>

I thought about that for a few seconds. It made me sick to cooperate with the Yeerk. But what other choice did I have? <Here are my terms: I will go outside. You hold the rope.>

The Yeerk laughed. <And when you reach the Time Matrix you'll activate it and disappear, leaving me behind.>

<No. I would not leave Loren . . . I mean, the humans. Search Alloran's mind. He knows. You'll see it's true.>

Visser Thirty-two considered for a moment. <Yes, it seems you are correct. Alloran decided you had formed some pathetic feelings for this human female. But just in case you decide to betray me anyway, I remind you that I still have my tail. I can finish your human friend slowly as we sink toward that black hole.>

It took a few minutes to tear enough cable loose from the controls to form a long lifeline. Even though I wouldn't weigh anything, I would still have mass enough to break a too-weak line.

True to his claim, Visser Thirty-two found four air hoods. They had been stashed in each of the individual quarters. They were simple but effective models. Basically, they were just clear plastic bags that slipped over your head and tied at the neck. There was a small oxygen bottle. Very small. The hoods were rated for five minutes. The mix of oxygen and other gases, as well as subtler ingredients, would keep my body from depressurizing in the vacuum of space.

But after five minutes my air would run out. The oxygen inside my body would expand, bursting every blood vessel, rupturing my eyes. A painful death.

I had not explained these details to Loren.

I tied the hood in place and helped Loren put hers on. We tied one on the still-unconscious Chapman. Then I carefully tied the cable around my tail.

<Ready?> the visser asked me.

<I'm ready,> I said. <You just worry about yourself, Yeerk.>

The visser laughed. <Alloran is so right about you. You're a moralizing, arrogant, weak-willed little fool.>

<Loren?> I said. <We're going to open the hatch. Air will rush out but we'll do it more slowly than before. Still, keep an eye on your fellow human. We don't want him sucked out into space.>

"We don't?" Loren asked.

I looked at her, puzzled.

"Sarcasm," she explained. "A type of humor."

I would have laughed, but I was just too scared. I lifted the hood and filled my lungs with cabin air. Then I replaced the hood, turned on the oxygen, and nodded to Visser Thirty-two.

The hatch began to open. Everything that could have been sucked out into space already had been, so nothing much happened. There was a sort of breeze, then nothing, as the hatch finished opening. But the cold was like a fist. Cold like nothing any planet dweller could imagine.

I stood in the doorway and stared out at space. Below me, huge beyond imagining, was the swirl of dust, feeding the black hole. At the far edge of the swirl was a star. The star was being drained by the black hole. A huge, long, arced plume of hot gas was being drawn from the star into the black hole.

I hoped there had not been planets around that star. I hoped no sentient species had met its fate this way, torn apart by the space-warping might of the black hole.

I had a vision of myself, falling away free. Falling and falling into the black monster. I shook my head to clear the image.

<Focus, Elfangor,> I muttered to myself. <Worry about the black hole if you fail. Not till then.>

I looked back along the axis of the *Jahar*. Her elongated oval and three rakish engines and wonderfully long shredder spike still looked so potent.

The ship spun in space. Around and around in a wobbly loop. It's disorienting, even if you've been through all the training for things like that. The swirl of dust and hot gases would be overhead one second, beneath me the next. Stars sped by overhead.

I searched back along the ship for the Time Matrix. But it wasn't there. Had it drifted entirely away? Had the living asteroids taken it?

Steadying myself as well as I could, I pushed off into space. I aimed to counter the spin of the ship. The result was that the ship now spun slowly beneath me. And there, rising from the far side of the ship, like a moon coming up over a planet, was the Time Matrix.

<I see it!> I reported. <It's wedged in place by the engine pylons. Going after it.>

If you have never tried to move in zero gravity, you have no idea how utterly impossible it can be. You're floating weightless, with no up or down. Nothing to push off against. If the cable were to break I could float forever, just a few feet away from the ship, and yet never be able to move back across that tiny distance.

But I had been well-trained in zero-gravity movement. I yanked lightly on the cable with my tail, drawing myself back toward the ship. I timed the impact carefully and tapped two hooves on the hull. Just enough to change my direction.

I floated back toward the engines. Back toward the Time Matrix. It lay there like the egg of some unimaginably huge bird. Ten feet across, it fit neatly into the cradle formed by the engine pylon.

I drifted toward it, stretching out hands stiff and numb with cold. I touched it! Touched it and stopped my momentum carefully so that I wouldn't bounce off it.

My bare, frozen hands touched the hard, smooth surface. And somehow, the Time Matrix seemed to warm me. I felt heat glow up through my stiff fingers and up my awkward arms.

Now how do I move you back to the hatch? I wondered.

It was far too big to get my arms around. I would have to use the cable to fashion a sling. And I had exactly three minutes before the hood ran empty and all of us — the visser, Loren, Chapman, and I — were done for.

I worked quickly, untying the cable from my tail, forming it into two big loops with a cross-brace. It wasn't much. It wasn't secure. But it was all I could do.

<Okay,> I said. <Pull!>

The visser pulled, and slowly the Time Matrix, with me holding onto one of the cable ends, began to move toward the hatch.

It's going to work, I told myself. *It's going to work. We are going to use the Time Matrix.*

The first living creatures to have used the dread machine for thousands and thousands of years.

chapter 3

We snugged the Time Matrix up against the hatch, with air and time running out.

Once more inside the *Jahar*, I could see the suffering that Loren had endured. The blend of gases from the hoods was adjusted for Andalite bodies, not humans. She was in pain from gradual decompression. She could barely stand.

The visser, though, still stood. Or at least floated.

<Well done, Andalite,> he said. <Thirty seconds left to activate this thing.>

<Go ahead, Yeerk,> I sneered. <Make your move.>

I saw the coldness in his eyes. Colder even than the freezing cold of space. I knew I had guessed right. He had intended to eliminate me. One slash of his Andalite tail to finish me off.

But I was prepared and he knew it. Which of us would win a tail fight in zero gravity? He didn't know, and neither did I. And there was no time left for mistakes.

How does one turn this thing on? I wondered, looking at the white globe half crammed into the hatchway. *No visible instruments or control panels. Has to be direct mind-link using a physical interface.*

Loren moved her lips as though speaking. But in the vacuum no sound could be heard. I saw through the plastic hood that her lips had turned blue. Her eyes were fluttering.

<Touch,> I said. <The Matrix responds to touch. I think if we touch and form a mental link, we can —>

The visser moved. Not to attack, but to press his hand against the Time Matrix. He was trying to gain control over it before I could!

I pressed my hand against the Matrix and searched desperately in my mind for a link.

What happened next is almost impossible to describe. And surely impossible for anyone to understand who has not experienced it himself.

As I touched the Time Matrix, and searched for it with my mind, the entire universe simply opened up. Opened up like a piece of fruit that has been exploded into its segments. But that's not telling a millionth of it.

Everything changed. Everything! The ship around me, the familiar *Jahar*, was suddenly not a vessel anymore, but an amazing array of fragments, each twisted inside out and outside in. Each piece was connected to every other piece in insane ways that no rational mind could make sense of.

And from each piece of the ship there stretched lines that curled and twirled through space, connecting back to the Taxxon world and back to the *StarSword* and back to a thousand other places, all somehow visible to me. I could see every place the ship had been. It was as if each of those places were right here and a billion miles away at once!

But all the lines of the ship were dim and dull compared to the spectacle of the living bodies around me. I saw the Andalite body of Alloran opened up and split apart, transparent, twisted so that every part could be seen from every angle at once. I saw the living, beating hearts! I saw the muscles of the tail. I saw the ways the eyes were attached to the brain, and not just from outside, but from inside.

And to my horror, I saw the Yeerk slug. It was wrapped around Alloran's brain, sinking into every wrinkle and crevice, sinking deep between the four segments. I could literally *see* the flow of thoughts and emotions. I saw inside the slug that was Visser Thirty-two. I saw the way the Yeerk mind drew memories from Alloran and sent back orders. I saw and felt the impotent rage of Alloran as he lay helpless in the Yeerk's grasp.

I know how impossible it is to really grasp this. But I saw in and through and around everything at once. I saw time lines stretching back from the Yeerk and back from Alloran. I saw their pasts. And I saw the horrible moment when those time lines became entwined, becoming one.

I could see Alloran's past in flashes of wild action and wild emotion. I saw the terrible moment when Alloran stood amidst battlefield slaughter on the Hork-Bajir home world. I saw the ground piled high with Hork-Bajir and Andalite dead.

And I saw the actual decision deep in Alloran's despairing brain, the decision to release the forbidden Quantum virus.

I felt his bitterness when even that evil measure failed, and the Hork-Bajir were lost to the Yeerks. I saw the retreat of the shattered, beaten Andalite force.

I was almost drowning from this assault of data. It was as if I had been plugged directly into every computer ever built and all of them were dumping information into my brain.

I even saw the time line of the black hole itself. I saw it form from the explosive moment of the universe's birth, and watched it condense and burn, bright as a huge star. I saw it die and collapse, digging a hole in space itself.

But then, amidst all the swarm of information, among all the insides and outsides, all the pasts and all the connections, I felt the will of Visser Thirty-two.

I felt him take hold of the Time Matrix. And I felt the Matrix respond, felt it turn to him. In the visser's Yeerk brain I saw the image of the Yeerk home world. He was forming it, clear and detailed.

I saw the awful pools where the Yeerks were born. I felt the Kandrona rays that beat down from the Yeerks' own strange sun.

He was directing the Time Matrix! Aiming it! Telling it to take him there, to the Yeerk home world!

NO!

I focused my will, and in the weird universe I inhabited, I saw my own living brain as it focused, concentrated, bringing more and more mental power to bear.

It was insane! I could watch my own brain work. Watch my own brain watching my own brain watching my own brain.

I had to take control of the Time Matrix. I had to fight, to resist the visser. I summoned up an image in my head. But it was a confused picture. I saw the part of the Andalite world where I had grown up. The trees, the grass, the sky. . . . But mixed in with that image were others. I saw them float up out of my own brain. I saw them skim by, three-dimensional pictures looking so flat and strange in this multidimensional universe.

I saw my own Andalite world, but mixed in with it were images of Earth — the pictures I had seen.

Somewhere far off, I realized I could see my own body beginning to freeze. Systems were shutting down. I could see inside fingers that were frozen stiff. I could see a tail that hung limp, all tension gone. My hearts were beating sluggishly.

I was watching my own body die. I was weakening. The visser, too, was hurt by the cold, but the Yeerk himself, down inside Alloran's head, was still alert and strong.

Slowly the balance shifted to him. The images were more and more of the Yeerk home world. His images were coming in over mine, like a tide. I was losing. I was failing as the cold shut down my body and reached tendrils into my mind.

And then . . . a new mind. Alien, but familiar in a way. I saw the Yeerk jerk in alarm and surprise. This new force, this new mind was strong. Stronger than he could have expected.

Loren!

I saw inside her and through her. I saw her thoughts. And I saw her push back the visser's own images. Not defeating him, but keeping him at bay.

I realized something else had changed. The black hole was further away now. The *Jahar* could still be seen, but it, too, was further away.

We were moving! The Time Matrix had been programmed, and we were moving through time.

The last memory I had, as the cold collapsed my consciousness, was of someone vast and incredible. A being like nothing I could have imagined. It saw me. It saw us all.

And it laughed.

chapter 4

I woke up with that laughter still ringing in my head.

I opened my main eyes and found to my surprise that I was standing. I opened my stalk eyes and looked around in all directions.

Trees. Grass. A stream running close by. A gentle breeze.

<Home? Am I home?>

I stared at a *therant* tree. The trunk. The branches. The vines. Impossible! It was *Hala Fala*! The oldest of the *therant* trees in the woods near my home. My father had shown me this tree when I was just a very small child. It was my *Garibah*. My Guide Tree.

I ground my hooves into the grass, taking a sample taste. Yes! It was the grass I had grown up on. The grass of home.

<How did I get here?> I wondered aloud.

I reached out with both hands and placed them on the smooth bark of *Hala Fala*. And I heard the "voice" of the tree, deep and simple and powerful.

It did not speak in words, of course. Only a handful of trees have ever used words, and even then, it could take them hours to say a single word. But *Hala Fala* spoke to me, as it usually did, letting me know that it felt my presence. Letting me feel its own strange, slow mind.

<I'm home,> I whispered to *Hala Fala*.

And then, after all that had happened, I broke down. I sobbed. I cried. I told my guide tree everything in a rush of disjointed emotion. Of course, not even a *Garibah* can understand stories of space travel, of aliens, of wars and terrible decisions.

But it could hear my shame. It could hear despair for poor, doomed Arbron. It could hear my cries of pain for all I had seen. It heard my fear.

The *Garibah* could not change what had happened. And it could not tell me that I was forgiven, or that all would be well now. I knew the ritual of forgiveness. <I have made right everything that can be made right, I have learned everything that can be learned, I have sworn not to repeat my error, and now I claim forgiveness.>

But I had not yet made right everything that could be made right. I had not yet learned to understand my own mistakes. I was not ready to swear I would not repeat those mistakes. Forgiveness for all my terrible failings was still a long way off.

But the *Garibah*, the tree named *Hala Fala*, heard me, heard my shame and rage. And being heard helped.

My sobbing quieted. I took my hands away from the tree's smooth bark.

I walked slowly away, crunching up the sweet grass of home and trying, with my exhausted mind, to make sense of what had happened.

Clearly I had used the Time Matrix to carry me through time and space. Without experiencing any passage of time, I was home. But home *when*? Was this a hundred years ago? A thousand? The *Garibah* had been alive for seven thousand years. It could be anywhere in that time span.

I remembered trying to turn the Time Matrix to my own visions. And I guess I had succeeded. All these trees, all this lush grass, the *kafit* bird that fluttered by overhead, the little *hoobers* that jumped on springy tendrils and stared at me from their comical bulging eyes, all this was home. My home.

And across that stream, and over that next rise, I would see my family home. Just ahead! I broke into a run. I leaped the stream, like I always did, and suddenly I had to be home. I didn't care what anyone said. I didn't care. I wanted my mother and father. I wanted to lie down in the deep grass of the scoop and find my old toys and be a child again.

I ran, flat-out, and yes, the slopes were so familiar! And yes, every tree was where it should be. I ran to the top of the rise, ready to look down into our neat, oval-shaped family scoop, and —

I stopped.

There it was: the scoop. The bowl dug out of the ground by my great-great-grandparents and planted with every delicious variety of grass and flowers. And there was the lodge, the blue-plex awning that covered the south quarter of the scoop and kept our things out of the rain.

But just behind the scoop, in a place it could not possibly be, was a waterfall.

It was an incredible waterfall. It fell hundreds of feet from the edge of a cliff. A cliff that simply stood there. No mountains on either side. Just a cliff that rose sharply up from the grass.

I felt a sick queasiness in my stomach.

I was seeing something I had seen before. It was the picture from what Loren had called a cigarette ad. But it was in a place it should not be. In a place it *could* not be. It was violating the very laws of physics.

This was not home.

I tore my gaze away from the impossible waterfall, and looked around. From the top of the rise I could see fairly far.

What I saw was impossibility piled on impossibility.

But what I focused on first was the sky.

It was a deep red and gold, like the red and gold of my own world. It was also light blue, with fluffy white clouds. And it was green.

Stretching over my head was a sky broken into jigsaw-puzzle fragments. Here a patch of Andalite sky. There a lighter blue. And over there, a shocking green torn by ragged bolts of electricity. Clouds drifted through the paler blue segments and then disappeared when they reached a different segment. Lightning in the green sky disappeared when it reached one of the other patches.

I had never known what the sky of Earth looked like, but now I could guess. It was pale blue, with fluffy white clouds.

And I had never known the sky of the Yeerk world, but now I could guess that, too. It was green and torn by bolts of electricity.

What have we done? I wondered.

And I remembered the laughter of that vast and strange being I had glimpsed.

chapter 5

I wandered, amazed and appalled, through a world that made no sense. The parts that were familiar just made other parts seem stranger.

My scoop was there, right where it should be. But no one was around. Not a single other Andalite. Not my father or my mother.

Why? Where was I? If this wasn't home, where was it?

I wandered through woods and across open fields that were familiar. But then, across a field I'd known all my life, I found a sharp line drawn. The grasses of home stopped abruptly. And on the other side everything turned brown and muddy gray and a red so dark it was almost black.

On one side of the line, my own world. On the other side of the line, wild, tall, spiky grass and trees that rose only a foot tall before spreading out horizontally for thirty or forty feet. If you could even call something like that a tree.

I was startled by something that reached up out of the ground with a soft SHLOOP! It was like a Taxxon tongue, almost. Ten feet long and dark red, it shot up from a hole in the ground. It seemed to lick the air in a slow, circular pattern, as if it was searching blindly for something. Then, after a few seconds, it SHLOOPED! back into the ground.

Ten feet away, another such tongue. This time it reached for a beast that walked past, hunched over. The beast had four thick legs toward the back and two turned-in legs forward, with no discernable head.

This lumbering creature wandered straight toward the flickering tongue and suddenly, fast as a tail, the tongue reached out and wrapped around the beast's hind legs. The beast let out a groan, although where that sound came from, since it seemed not to have a head, was a mystery to me.

The tongue drew the beast toward its hole. But it could not suck the animal down, so it simply held it prisoner as the beast groaned.

The sky directly over that dark, unnerving landscape was dirty green and veined with silent lightning. It looked altogether like one of the fantasy-monster lands in fables that Andalite parents tell their little children about.

· I felt sick twisting inside me. I had never been to the Yeerk world, of course. But already I was beginning to guess what had happened. And I was sure that this blasted, vile, and empty landscape was the Yeerk home world.

Or at least the Yeerk home world as Visser Thirty-two saw it.

<The Time Matrix! Where is the Time Matrix?> I asked myself. It was the key. The Matrix had caused all this. The Matrix had created this awful place without logic or reason. And only through the Matrix could I escape.

<Loren. Where is she?>

I looked up at the sky and saw the patches of lighter, paler blue. The blue of Earth's sky. She would be beneath one of those patches of Earth blue. I was confident of that.

But which patch?

The waterfall. That was the place to start. It was the tallest thing around.

I turned my back on that depressing Yeerk vision and ran back toward the empty mockery of my home scoop. It was hard to look at that familiar area and accept the fact that it wasn't really my home.

Visser Thirty-two! It hit me like a shock from one of those Yeerk lightning bolts. If I was here, and perhaps even Loren was here, then so was he. Somewhere. Maybe within the confines of his Yeerk world, but maybe not!

If I could go looking for Loren, so could he. And if he found her first . . .

I saw the towering cliff from which the waterfall dropped and raced toward it, desperate now to find Loren. I ran flat-out. As I ran, I ate. It felt so good. Whatever else might be strange and unreal, the grass was good and familiar. And as it traveled up my legs from my hooves, I felt my strength growing.

I reached the pool where the water crashed in a huge white explosion. As I drew closer, I saw that the woods surrounding that pool were split into three different sections. The familiar Andalite trees filled a third or so. And different, but still lovely trees and green grass, covered another third. Around still another third was more of the dark Yeerk landscape.

It was all utterly impossible, of course. But still, standing beneath that massive waterfall, feeling the cold spray on my face, it was beautiful, too.

"Elfangor!"

I turned my stalk eyes and saw her. Relief flooded through me. <Loren! You're here!>

"Yeah. I'm here, all right. But where is *here*?"

<Wait. I'll come to you.>

I went toward her, threading my way around bushes and trees. And she came running toward me. She threw her strong human arms around my shoulders. And even though touching is more of a human thing than an Andalite thing, it wasn't so bad.

"Man, I thought I was all alone here," Loren said.

<No. I am here.>

"I would swear this was Earth, only look at the sky. It's all in patches. And some of those patches are very weird."

She released her hold on me, and after a second or two, I realized I should do the same.

<Have you looked around at all?>

She shook her head. It's something humans do to answer no. "I woke up over there, a few hundred feet back in the woods. Elfangor, it's exactly like this area of the park back home. There's a park where I play softball."

<Yes. It would be familiar to you. And there will probably be other familiar parts. Places you know. Maybe we could go and look around, now that we are together.>

She cocked her head sideways and looked at me. "You're still worried, aren't you?"

<There were three of us who made contact with the Time Matrix. You, me, and Visser Thirty-two.>

She twisted her human lips into a grimace. Then she looked skyward. "Those patches of green sky with the lightning. That's because of him, isn't it? Somehow, we made this place. The three of us. We created this place."

I stared at her in astonishment. There was no way she could begin to know about the physics of the Time Matrix. And yet she had reached the same conclusion as I had.

I laughed. Maybe Loren didn't understand the physics of the Time Matrix. But then again, neither did I. Neither did any Andalite, as far as I knew. Compared to the creatures who had created the Time Matrix, humans and Andalites were equally primitive.

<What do you think happened?> I asked Loren.

She smiled. "You're asking me?" She shrugged. "Well, that time machine — the Time Matrix, or whatever you call it — is not just like some car you drive through time. I think to steer it you have to imagine the place and time where you want to go. I think with three of us each having different ideas of where we wanted to go, well, this is the result: part me, part you, part . . . part *him*."

I saw that her eyes were staring past me. I adjusted my stalk eyes to follow the direction of her gaze.

There, standing on the far side of the pool, was Visser Thirty-two. The abomination.

But Visser Thirty-two was not standing alone.

chapter 6

Visser Thirty-two stood on the bank of the pool in the Yeerk zone, under his own green sky.

And on either side of him stood a creature like nothing I had ever seen or imagined. They were each about three feet tall and four and a half feet long. They were mostly a dark, dirty yellow with irregular black spots. But the head and shoulders were the deep red of the Yeerk plants.

The heads were tiny for the bodies, elongated, almost needle-sharp. The mouths were long and narrow. Hundreds of tiny, bright red teeth stuck out, jagged and wildly different in length and shape.

But what struck me as strangest was that the creatures did not have legs in the usual sense. They had wheels.

Yes, wheels. Four of them, to be exact.

The wheels were located where legs should be. Each was sloppy and irregular in shape, not perfectly round. But it was easy to see that the wheels were for real. There was mud and dirt all around them, and when I strained my stalk eyes I could even see where the creatures had left tracks in the dirt. Wheel tracks.

"Elfangor, what are those things?"

<I have no idea. I can't imagine what evolutionary path would conceivably have created a creature with wheels.>

Visser Thirty-two actually gave a jaunty wave of his hand. <So, young Elfangor, we meet again. As you see, I brought my pets: Jarex and Larex. And you brought your pet, too. Your pet human.>

Loren looked at me. In a voice Visser Thirty-two was sure to hear, she muttered, "You know, Elfangor, I'm beginning to see why you Andalites really dislike Yeerks. Whatever body they may be in, they still have the manners of slugs."

<Brave little human girl,> the Yeerk visser mocked. <Do you understand that even now my people are on their way to evaluate your primitive world? Do you understand that within a few years your people, you humans, will be slaves of the Yeerk Empire?>

"Blah, blah, blah," Loren said.

I had no idea what that meant. Neither did the visser.

"You do a lot of talking for a slug," Loren clarified. "You think I'm scared of you?"

<Yes. I know you're scared of me.>

For a moment Loren said nothing, but her lower lip was trembling slightly. Then, she knelt quickly, plunged her hand into the water, and withdrew it. She was holding a rock. She drew her arm back, swept her arm in a big loop, and released the rock with precise timing. The rock flew through the air at an impressive speed.

And the aim wasn't bad, either.

BONK!

<Ahhh!> the visser cried. The rock had struck him right in the face, just below his left main eye.

I don't know who was more amazed, me or the visser.

<What . . . what do you call that?> I asked her.

"That? We call that softball. I pitch for Frank's Pro Shop Twins back home. All-city two years in a row."

<What is softball?>

"It's a game we play."

<And you hit people in the face with rocks?>

"Not usually."

I was impressed by the human ability to throw things with such force. I was sure that Andalite scientists would enjoy studying humans someday. They appeared more frail and ridiculous than they were.

The visser was not impressed. He was just angry.

<So. You propel rocks at me! You'll be very sorry you ever propelled a rock at me, human. Jarex! Larex! Attack!>

The situation stopped being amusing very quickly. The twin beasts turned their wheels, sluggishly at first. But then picked up speed.

I almost didn't move, I was so fascinated seeing the biological wheels turn. It was truly incredible.

<You admire my pets, Andalite? They are a species called Mortrons. As a young lieutenant I went on a survey party to a world that was later destroyed when its sun went nova. We thought we might be able to make Controllers of these Mortrons, but that didn't work out. Their brains are simply too tiny to accommodate us. Instead, I brought two of them home as pets.>

All the while the visser talked — or "blah, blah, blahed," as Loren had said — the Mortrons gathered speed and raced around the circumference of the pool.

They made a strange sound. A HUF-HUF-HUF-HUF. Faster and faster.

<They have amazing capacities, my young friend Elfangor. As you will soon see.>

<What's the matter, Yeerk? Afraid to fight me tail-to-tail?> I taunted. I hoped the answer was yes, because I was not at all sure which of us would win a tail fight. While I *was* totally confident I could deal with these Mortrons.

HUF-HUF-HUF-HUF-HUF!

The wheels spun faster, and the ungainly yellow and black monstrosities were nearly to the edge of the Yeerk portion of the pool. I watched carefully to see whether they could move from the Yeerk area into the human area.

Unfortunately, the answer was yes.

<Don't worry,> I told Loren. <I can handle these two creatures.>

HUF-HUF-HUF-HUF-SCRINK-SHWOOOP!

Suddenly the creatures each split into two parts! The bottom portion, the yellow part with the wheels, swerved away. The dark red upper portion simply rose from the body, unfolded leathery wings I'd never even suspected, and flew straight at me!

"Elfangor!" Loren cried.

<Hah-hah! Kill, Jarex! Kill, Larex! Kill the Andalite!> Visser Thirty-two cackled gleefully.

The first Mortron — I don't know if it was Jarex or Larex — opened its mouth and showed its rows of uneven but brutally unpleasant teeth. It powered through the air like a rocket.

I dodged left and struck with my tail blade!

FWAPP!

SPLEET! FLUMP. FLUMP.

My tail blade sliced the Mortron into two chunks. The two separate pieces fell to the ground with a wet splat.

"Elfangor, the other one!"

The second Mortron used the distraction provided by his brother to swoop wide, then arch in behind me. A tactic that would have worked on most opponents. But not on an Andalite who can see in all directions at once.

His toothy mouth was inches from my neck when I struck.

FWAPP!

SPLEET! FLUMP. FLUMP.

And the second Mortron bird-portion fell in pieces to the ground.

I was feeling pretty good, until I looked at the visser and saw the amusement in his eyes.

"Elfangor, look. Look!" Loren cried.

I turned my stalk eyes toward the ground. With amazing speed, the two bloody halves of each Mortron were growing. One piece of each was growing to become a complete bird-portion again. And the other piece was going even further — growing into a complete, two-piece, yellow and black, four-wheeled Mortron.

I had sliced both Mortrons in half. And now they were becoming four Mortrons.

<Are you doing the math in your head, Elfangor?> the visser jeered. <They regenerate! Cut an attacking Mortron in pieces and each piece grows again to become a complete Mortron. It's the killing

frenzy. It gives them an enzyme boost that makes them regenerate! Try to kill these four and you'll have eight. Kill those eight and you'll have sixteen! Thirty-two! Sixty-four!>

I stared in horror as the Mortron pieces grew and grew. In seconds they would be ready to attack again. And anything I did to destroy them would merely make more of them!

<Loren, I don't know what to do. If only I had a shredder!>

"Can you outrun them?"

<Yes, I can. But you can't! They are faster than you are. And I won't leave you.>

"You won't have to. Maybe. How strong is your back? Never mind, it must be strong enough. Elfangor, don't be offended, okay?"

<Offended by what?>

"Hold still. I'm gonna try something."

She came to me and placed one hand on the back of my neck. She placed another hand on my rump, right at the base of my tail. And suddenly, she leaned her weight on me, swung one leg up and over, and came to rest straddling my back. She sat there with one human leg hanging off either side of my back and held her hands clasped around my neck.

I turned my stalk eyes around and found myself staring directly into her small blue human eyes.

"Now let's run," she said.

<With you on my back?>

But even while I was standing there in blank astonishment, I saw a fully formed Mortron rise from the dirt. It was just a few feet away and it launched its bird-part. Leather wings propelled jagged razor-sharp teeth straight for my throat.

"Elfangor, this is not the time to think," Loren yelled. "Run! Ruuuuun!"

So I did. With the human girl actually on my back, I ran.

chapter 7

We ran. Or I ran, and Loren rode lightly on my back. And we quickly outran the visser's beasts. Those biological wheels were swift, but not as swift as an Andalite's hooves.

As for the visser, he chose not to give chase. At least not just then. But I knew I had not seen the end of him.

We left the "Andalite" portion of this new universe and ran through an increasingly strange environment.

The sky overhead was blue, but darkening just a bit.

The woods gave way to a cluttered landscape filled up with manufactured things. The grass under my hooves became a hard, gray-black substance. White stripes lined the middle.

<What is this thing we are on?> I asked.

"It's a street," Loren said.

<What does it do?>

"Well, remember that Mustang you were driving around on the Taxxon world? Streets are what Mustangs travel on."

As soon as she said it I could see how sensible it was. Of course. This way the human "cars" — which is how, Loran informed me, humans commonly refer to these machines — would not damage tasty grass.

On both sides of the street there were cars sitting. Beyond the cars, further back from the street were rectangular boxy structures. They were quite large and decorated with small squares and rectangles of transparent material. The tops were angled and covered in reddish-orange or dark gray scales.

<Are these human creations?>

"Yep. These are houses. That's what we live in."

<You live in them? How?>

"Um, well . . . I mean, you go in through the front door. See? The tall rectangles on the front of each house? You go in through those."

<Inside.>

"Yes, inside."

<Ah! Wait! You mean these structures are hollow!>

"Of course they're hollow. Pretty soon we'll be to my house. Then I'll show you. You'll meet my mom. You can see my room."

I didn't know what to say to that. My own home scoop had been empty. My mother and father had not been there. I doubted that Loren's mother would be in her house. But I wasn't sure.

<Don't expect too much,> I warned.

"She'll be there," Loren said forcefully. "Next house. The one with the bushes out front."

I had very little experience understanding the expression of human voices, but I sensed fear in Loren's voice. Uncertainty.

I stopped before her house. There was a very attractive patch of grass in the front. Obviously, humans grow their own food in neatly cultivated squares in front of each house.

<You must have very hardy grasses to be able to feed whole families and still look so perfect and so green.>

"What?" Loren asked.

She frowned and I let the matter drop. I was sure now that she was worried. She slid from my back.

<I'll wait while you go inside your hollow house,> I said.

"No. Come with me, Elfangor. Hold my hand."

I held her hand and she walked up a series of four steps. I wondered about the steps. Were they a way to slow down any approaching enemy, so that no one could charge directly inside the hollow house?

With her free hand Loren twisted a metallic ball. The door opened a little and Loren pushed it open all the way.

She was correct. The house was hollow inside. In fact, now I could see that the outer walls were no more than a few inches thick. But inside the hollowness were other walls, with other doors. It was like a maze!

Lights glowed from the flat covering above us. Other lights were hung on the walls. The floor was covered with a sort of very short, pale tan grass. I tried to taste some of it, but my hooves could not eat it.

"Mom?" Loren said in a loud, quavering voice.

"I'm in here, honey."

I felt Loren's hand jerk in surprise. Then she let go of my hand and ran along the strange inedible tan grass and turned out of sight through a rectangular opening.

I followed slowly, unsure of myself. I did not know any human rituals. I knew what I would have said when first meeting an Andalite friend's parents, but I'd never met a human's parents.

I heard Loren sob. "Mommy!"

I turned the corner and looked into another of the mazelike rooms. This room had metallic devices against one wall, all rectangular and white. Humans are very partial to rectangles. The floor was smooth here, and slippery for my hooves.

Loren was wrapped in the arms of another human. This new human was also female, as far as I could tell. She had hair the same color as Loren's, but dark brown eyes. Perhaps that was a sign of age. Perhaps humans have blue eyes till a certain age. Or until they reproduce and have children.

I wanted to ask Loren if my guess was correct, but Loren's mother was looking at me with her brown eyes.

"Loren, honey, shouldn't you introduce your friend?"

Loren frowned. She looked at me, then back at her mother. "Mom, this is Elfangor. Don't be afraid, okay? He's my friend."

The human woman smiled. "Now, why would I be afraid? I like meeting your friends. You know that."

"But . . . Mom . . . Elfangor's not exactly one of my school friends."

"I like meeting your friends."

Loren's face was growing pale. She darted worried eyes at me and back to her mother. "Mom, can't you tell that Elfangor is not a normal friend from school? Can't you tell that he's different?"

"Oh, honey." The woman laughed. "He's just an Andalite like any other."

Loren jumped back like she'd been slapped. I swept the room with my stalk eyes, ready for trouble. I cocked my tail and waited, tense and confined in the narrow room with the slippery floor.

"What do you mean, he's an Andalite? You don't know about Andalites! You *can't* know about Andalites."

Loren's mother made a face. "You know, just because I'm your mother doesn't mean I'm an antique! I do keep up with things, Miss Modern. Your generation thinks it invented *everything*. You think you kids invented Andalites? We had Andalites when I was your age, too."

"How do you know about Andalites?!" Loren yelled. There was water leaking from her eyes. "Oh, God, you're not real! You're not real!"

"Now, Loren, if you are going to treat me disrespectfully, I am going to send you to your room."

"You're not my mother! You're not *real*!"

I placed a hand on Loren's shoulder. By now I had learned that humans like to be touched when they are upset. <Loren, you're right. She is not your mother. She's something you made out of your own thoughts and memories of your mother. She knows about Andalites because you knew about Andalites when you imagined her.>

But Loren did not want to be comforted. She threw off my hand. She turned to me with her face red, and water flowing from her blue eyes. And she screamed. "Get away from me! Get away from me! This is all your fault! Just leave me alone!"

She pushed past me and ran from the hollow house, sobbing loudly.

I was alone with the artificial mockery of a human woman. <I am sorry.>

"Would you like some pop and cookies?" the human woman asked.

<No, thank you,> I said. I wondered what I should do. I didn't know how to comfort a human girl who is trapped inside a nightmare. <Loren's mother, can you show me where Loren's room is?>

"Up the stairs, on the right. But leave the door open a crack. That's the rule in our house when Loren has Andalites over to play."

chapter 8

I felt that Loren needed a little time alone. It was dangerous letting her walk around by herself. But I couldn't force her to talk to me when she was angry and afraid.

I had to climb many stairs to reach Loren's room. I still didn't understand the point of stairs. I guess humans just love anything with straight edges and a rectangular shape. The stairs were definitely rectangular. And they allowed the humans to place a second level in their houses. This made the house a larger rectangle. And I suppose this is important in some way.

Inside Loren's room was a long rectangle covered with artificial skin. I suspect she used it for sleeping. I had seen that when she slept, she lay flat and stretched out straight. There were two other flat rectangles, one mostly covered with bound papers. The bound papers were called books or magazines. Loren had explained them to me. A sort of extremely primitive computer file.

I opened one of them. There were words printed on the pages but the words stopped abruptly in the middle of the book. Of course. Loren had not finished the book. So she could not recreate it out of her memory.

There was a small picture of Loren with two other people. All were making human smiles. One was her mother. The other I believed was male. Perhaps her father.

I took this picture and held it in my hand. I looked around the room, trying to understand this alien girl. But alien things are hard to make sense of.

By the time I got out of the hollow house and back to the street, Loren was gone from sight. I worried about finding her. But after wandering the alien landscape for a while, I heard a far-off sound. A THWACK!

I ran at top speed to the sound and found Loren in a field of short grass and dirt. She stood with her back to a high wire cage. In her right hand she held a sort of long, shaped stick, wider at the far end. With her left she tossed a round white sphere up in the air. And then, quickly clasping the stick with both hands, she swung the stick till it struck the falling white sphere.

The result was fascinating. The sphere went flying through the air.

Loren watched the sphere until it fell to the grass, perhaps a hundred feet away. Then she reached down into a bucket by her feet, lifted out a second, identical sphere, and repeated the entire process.

<Loren!>

She ignored my approach.

Toss . . . swing . . . THWACK!

The sphere flew over the grass and landed at the edge of a narrow band of trees.

Toss . . . swing . . . THWACK!

<Loren?>

"See, *this* is softball," she said, without looking at me. "See that high spot there? That's the pitcher's mound. The pitcher throws the ball across this plate. The batter swings and tries to knock the stitches off her."

<Off the pitcher?>

Toss . . . swing . . . THWACK!

"That was my last ball. I'd better go retrieve them. Our coach goes ape if we lose equipment."

She started off across the field, still carrying her shaped stick.

<You are upset,> I said.

"What was your first clue?"

<This all seems very bizarre to you. Me as well.>

"Bizarre? My neighborhood with no people in it? My mom sounding like a dimwit robot but knowing things she can't possibly know? The sky in patches?"

<Is that humor?>

"It's sarcasm," she said. We reached one of the white balls. She picked it up and used the stick to knock it back toward the tall wire cage.

I held the small picture out for her to see. <I got this from your room. I thought you might like something personal. I don't know if we will be able to go back to your house. >

"That is *not* my house," she said. But she took the picture and stared at it. Her face seemed to grow softer. Her mouth corners became more nearly level. Her forehead skin grew less wrinkled. "Elfangor, what is happening here?"

<What you said earlier, more or less. I think that in order to direct the Time Matrix you need to form a mental image of where and when you want to go. We couldn't do that because all three of us were fighting for control. We each — you, me, Visser Thirty-two — had ideas of where to go. You wanted your home. I wanted mine. I guess he wanted his. Nobody's vision was complete. We

were all freezing and suffocating for lack of air. The Time Matrix did the best it could.>

"I thought it was supposed to be a time machine."

I sighed. <Some people believe that there is not just one universe, but many. Maybe, somehow, instead of traveling through the time and space of our own universe, we forced the Time Matrix to create a whole new universe. When the three of us wrestled for control, the Time Matrix could not make sense of what we were asking it to do. So it created this place.>

Loren resumed walking toward the far edge of the field. She stooped to pick up another ball and knocked it back in the direction we'd come from. "So my mom. My mother . . . she's just made up out of my memories."

<And even then, not all your memories. She is not complete. She is bits and pieces of your memories of her. I think the more complicated things, like sentient creatures, are probably the most likely to be incomplete.>

Loren made a snorting sound. "Great universe, isn't it?"

<That was sarcasm, too?>

"Yeah. That was sarcasm, too."

We had reached the trees. Loren plunged in. "Look how complete all the trees are. Why are the grass and the trees and the air all like they should be?"

<Because a person . . . whether it's an Andalite or a human, is a thousand times more complicated than a tree.>

I noticed that Loren was not looking at me. Instead she was staring alertly into the woods.

<Do you see something?>

"No. I . . . I have a feeling, is all. I have to go look."

I followed her through the woods. We traveled no more than fifty feet when we reached what Loren had sensed.

The trees stopped abruptly. The sky above us stopped, too. The ground and the grass all stopped. Just stopped. And beyond it was blank whiteness.

The pure, blank, white of Zero-space. Nothingness.

I felt awed and frightened all at once. We were standing at the edge of our tiny universe. Loren reached toward the whiteness, stretching her hand out beyond the edge of soil and vegetation, air and sky.

Her arm reached that edge and curved back on itself. It simply bent in a perfect arc, so that her hand was reaching back toward her own face.

"Noooooooo!" she screamed. "No! No! No!"

<Loren, it's only . . .> Only what? What could I say to comfort her when I felt my own mind spinning out of control?

She turned to me, eyes wide and reddish now. "I want to go home, Elfangor. I want to go home! This place is wrong. It's wrong!"

<I know. I feel it, too.>

"We have to get out of here. This place can't exist. Feel it. It's wrong!"

<We have to find the Time Matrix,> I said. <It's the only way. But we don't know where it is. And Visser Thirty-two will try to stop us.>

She was still holding the shaped stick. The softball stick. She looked at me with cold fury in her blue human eyes. And I saw something there that almost scared me.

She clutched the stick tightly. "Let him try and stop us. Let him try."

chapter 9

We wandered around the edge of our new universe, keeping the blank whiteness on our right as we went.

We traveled along the outer rim of the Earth portion of the universe. But even there at the outer rim, this new universe was not consistent. As we walked we came across small areas, sometimes no more than twenty feet across, where we'd suddenly find Andalite life-forms or Yeerk life-forms. The Andalite patches were harder to notice since they were not so different from the Earthlike areas. But the patches of Yeerk environment were like open sores.

We skirted around the Yeerk patches. Most of the Earth environment was made up of woods and grass fields. But here and there were human buildings as well. We saw the street where Loren lived. And we saw her school — a squat, ugly box made of thousands of small reddish-brown rectangles called bricks.

"I can't believe I brought the school building into this universe, but I forgot to bring a grocery store."

<What is a grocery store?>

"A place to buy food."

<Ah.> I had seen Loren eat aboard the *Jahar*, of course. She and the other human had eaten emergency rations of liquefied grass. The rations we give Andalites who are too sick or injured to stand up and eat normally.

We walked along a street that appeared in the middle of a field. The street merely began, ran for a few hundred feet, and ended. It made Loren anxious, I could tell. She explained that the street didn't belong there.

But then we saw a building decorated with two yellow arcs.

"Can't be!" Loren gasped. "No way! It's Mickey D's! I brought a McDonald's here!"

She broke into a run and I followed her. We entered the hollow building. Inside there was a single human. But he was not like any human I had ever seen.

"Oh, God, what did I do?" Loren cried. She placed her hand over her mouth.

I had never seen this human gesture, but I knew she was horrified. You see, the human looked like any normal human. Except that his face was covered with red splotches and pustules. And he had no eyes. No eyes at all.

But he could speak.

"Welcome to McDonald's. May I take your order?"

"Oh, no. No," Loren wailed.

"Would you like fries with that? Or a hot apple pie?"

<Is this a human you know?> I asked.

"No. I mean, yes. He's this guy who works at McDonald's and he always waits on us when we go for burgers after a game. My friend Jennifer says he likes me. But all I ever notice is how bad his acne is. The poor guy. The poor guy."

<The food he has may still be real,> I suggested. <It would help you to eat some human food.>

She seemed ready to run from the place. But in the end, hunger won out over horror. Loren steeled herself and walked back to the eyeless human.

"Welcome to McDonald's. May I take your order?"

"Yes. I mean . . . yes. I'd like a Big Mac, fries, and a Coke."

"That'll be four dollars and nineteen cents."

Loren hesitated. But then she reached into a flap of her artificial skin and pulled out some crumpled pieces of paper and some round metallic objects. She handed all this to the eyeless human.

Somehow the human managed to take the paper and metal. Although how he did it without eyes was a mystery. This universe we had created had strange rules.

The eyeless human placed several objects into a bag. They smelled strange and foul to me. But Loren looked in the bag and smiled.

"Well, I did one thing right when I created this universe. I put extra pickles on the Big Macs. Come on. Let's go back outside. I don't want to eat with . . . with *him*."

"Enjoy your meal, and come again!" the sad monstrosity said.

We went back outside and Loren found a place to sit on the grass and began to devour her food. Watching creatures with mouths eat can be disturbing. Especially when you discover some of the things they eat. Between huge gulping, slobbering bites with her flashing white teeth and grinding jaws, Loren told me what a "Big Mac" was. I'd rather not have known.

But the human food revived Loren. She had her old energy back. And even her sense of humor.

"At least I didn't try and recreate the cheerleading squad in this universe," she said. "They rejected me, and I'd hate to think what kind of mess I'd have made of some of them."

I didn't understand what she was talking about, but I understood that she was feeling better. I gazed up at the weird, patchy sky, and around at the disjointed landscape. Then, suddenly, it hit me.

<It's a multidimensional pattern!> I said.

"Huh?" Loren asked, attempting to form words, even though her mouth was filled with two-inch-long, pale yellow sticks called "french fries."

<The sky, the way little bits of Andalite and Yeerk environments are mixed in with Earth environments. And probably the other way around, too. I didn't see it at first, but there is a pattern. It just seems strange because it makes sense in higher dimensions, but not in three dimensions. But I am sure now. It's a hyper spiral.>

Loren swallowed. "A what?"

<A spiral. But in extra dimensions. And if I'm right . . . yes! The Time Matrix will be at the center of the spiral!>

"Which is where?" Now Loren was sucking liquid into her mouth through a tube that inserted into a cylinder filled with brown water.

<I'm not sure. But I think I can find it. And if I can find it, so can that Yeerk!>

Loren jumped up. "That's why he hasn't tried to track us down. He's after the Time Matrix! Let's go. Let's go!"

<You seem to have recovered.>

Loren pointed at the cylinder of liquid. "Sugar rush, Elfangor. Let's go before it wears off."

chapter 10

I led the way toward what I hoped was the center of this universe. The patches of sky grew more varied over our heads. And the patches of different environments grew more numerous. Soon we were walking through a place that was only half Earth, with the rest divided between gentle Andalite countryside and harsh Yeerk lands.

"I like your planet, from what I've seen of it," Loren said. "It's like Earth, only without the houses and buildings. But you must have cities and all somewhere. I mean, you build spaceships. You have incredible technology."

<Long ago we had cities,> I explained. <But we were free-roaming herd animals to begin with. I mean, that's how we evolved. Millions of years ago Andalites moved in vast herds, which would split off into smaller herds at different times of the year. Then, gradually, we got used to forming smaller herds. Families, really.

Each family made its scoop, and we each held our own grazing lands. All this Andalite environment you see is part of my family's grazing land.>

We came to a patch of Yeerkish territory and skirted around the blackened vegetation and sluggish pools. On the other side was a wide band of Andalite land which we walked through.

<Once we evolved to form families, we began to study science and nature. And again, over millions of years, we learned to build things. You know — weapons and vehicles that let us fly over the land. And communicators for extending the reach of thought-speak. Scoops became larger. Families joined with other families. Building grew. Soon we had thousands of Andalites all crammed together without enough grazing space. But we were learning space travel at the same time. Still, we weren't happy. We knew something was wrong. We broke down our cities, divided the land, and went back to life in simple family scoops. We kept building spaceships, but we did it in little bits and pieces, here and there, spread out through the tens of thousands of scoops. My own family does some of that. We design heat transfer components for fight-

ers. Another family builds the pieces from our designs. Another family transports the pieces to the spaceport. I guess the three spaceports are about as close as we come to what you would call a city now.>

"We're very different, aren't we?" Loren said. She sounded sad.

<Yes. In some ways. But not so very different in others.>

"When all this is done, you'll go back to your planet. I'll go back to mine. And you'll erase all my memories of this."

I was startled by the idea. <Loren, we no longer have the *Jahar*. Or any ship. I can't erase your memories without that technology.>

"But if you could, you would?"

I hadn't thought about it. But suddenly I realized the truth. It shocked me. <No. I wouldn't.>

"Why not?"

<Because . . . because I don't think after all that's happened I could stand to be the only person alive who knew the truth. And I don't think I could stand having you forget me, Loren.>

Loren nodded. She smiled. "I care about you, too, Elfangor. I care a lot."

I was puzzled. Had I said I cared about her? No. Not in those words. And yet I did. I did care about this alien who no longer seemed so alien.

<We would be able to move faster if you climbed on my back as you did before,> I suggested.

"I guess we would."

She climbed on my back and I set off at a run. I was confident now that I knew the pattern of this universe. And I was fairly sure that we would find the Time Matrix at the very center of the swirl. But would we find that Visser Thirty-two had solved the puzzle before us?

The different environments were broken into smaller and smaller patches, and now there was a roughly equal amount of each of the three planets. It became more and more difficult to go around the Yeerk areas.

We came to one Yeerk area that stretched directly across our path. <I think we should go through it,> I said.

I stepped gingerly into the Yeerk area. Instantly the air was warmer, almost stifling. Humidity shot up so that my fur clung to me.

I closed my hooves to the sparse Yeerk vegetation. I didn't trust those dark red plants. A bright tongue shot up from the ground, as I had seen happen before. It licked the air, searching for us, but these creatures or plants — or whatever they were — were used to slower prey. I easily stepped out of its range.

A pall settled over us as we crossed a landcape that seemed designed to be depressing. And then, at last, we reached good Andalite grass again. Grass and trees and the scoop of a friend I had known all my life.

"Is that your home?"

<No. It's the scoop of a friend's family.>

"Maybe your friend is around."

<That's what scares me. Your mother . . . that McDonald person . . . I don't want to see my friend that way.>

Suddenly I stumbled. My right forehoof had caught on a rock.

"Elfangor! Elfangor! Something is happening!" Loren cried. "My fingernails! They're growing!"

She held up her hands so that my back-turned stalk eyes could see them. The hard portion at the end of her human fingers had grown half an inch.

<Your hair is growing, too,> I said.

She felt it. "My God, it's grown an inch. It's like it would grow in a few weeks!"

<My hooves are growing, too. That's why I tripped. It's something I was afraid of. As we get closer to the center of this swirl universe, time is accelerating. We are going to age faster than normal.>

"Then we'd better hurry!"

I redoubled my speed, careful to lift my scruffy hooves well clear on each step.

The entire false universe was coming together now. There were no longer clearly different patches of Andalite, human, or Yeerk terrain. Trees and grass, scoop and house, and sludgy natural Yeerk pools all seemed to meld together.

It was like walking through a surreal nightmare. The sky itself seemed to swoop down, to gather and swirl in patterns of dark blue, light blue, and lightning-wracked green.

"Okay, now this is weird," Loren said. But her voice, too, seemed to swirl into patterns that made it sound musical and strange.

I tripped and fell forward, throwing Loren free. My hooves had become totally unmanageable. I whipped my tail blade forward and quickly trimmed my hooves. It was a rough job, and as soon as I had cut away the excess, they began growing out again.

I looked at Loren and had to stop myself from crying out. Her fingernails were two inches long! Her toenails were sticking through the fabric of her artificial hooves! And her golden hair was so long it reached to the ground.

She stumbled forward, pointing. "Look! Look!"

I had already seen what she was just noticing: the swirling tornado that was the very center of our universe. It was a vortex, a tornado made up of the very substance of our three worlds. Sky and soil and living things all swirled insanely around us.

"Look out!" Loren ducked her head as something that looked like a human house, twisted and stretched, whipped by us.

<The Time Matrix! It should be in there!> I cried.

"In *there*? How can we go in there? It's impossible!"

<It's the only way. The Time Matrix is either in there or . . . or there's nothing beyond that swirl but emptiness and we'll be trapped inside that vortex forever.>

"Nice choice," Loren said. "And by the way, that was sarcasm, too."

<Yes, I'm beginning to recognize it,> I said. <We have to close our eyes. Block out

everything you see, or think you see, and dive in.>

"Take my hand, Elfangor."

I did. And together we pushed forward into a vortex made up of the very substance of time and space. A swirl of raw space-time.

chapter 11

Into the vortex.

I had no idea what I would find inside that awesome swirl. But then, I had long ago given up thinking I knew what would happen next. Everything had been a surprise since that day, not at all long ago, when Arbron and I were called to see the captain on the bridge of the *StarSword*.

Loren and I pushed forward. There was a feeling of resistance, as if a strong wind was holding us back. But at the same time, I felt that this resistance could be overcome.

The wind stopped and instead we were drawn forward. Drawn deep into the vortex. Everything swirled and swam around me. Vision was wild and distorted and filled with insane colors and bits and pieces of floating, oddly shaped matter.

Trees and buildings and creatures that seemed solid simply blew through us as if they were ghosts. Or as if *we* were ghosts.

And then we were through. In an instant, the swirling stopped. We were standing on a flat, featureless area no more than a hundred feet across. There was no vegetation. There was no detail. The sky was blanked out by the swirl that raged above and around us.

"The eye of the hurricane," Loren whispered.

I didn't understand what she said, but I understood what we both felt. We had penetrated a storm that twisted time and space.

And there, standing alone and pristine, was the Time Matrix. A simple, off-white sphere that had the power to create this eerie universe from our own imperfect thoughts.

<We did it,> I marveled. <The Time Matrix! It *is* here!>

"Yeah. Now what do we do about it? Look at my hair. Look at my fingernails. The distortion is really strong here, close like this."

<Yes. But we'll be fine once we contact the Matrix and get out of here.>

From the swirl wall I saw a head emerge, pressing forward into the empty field.

An Andalite head.

"It's him!"

The visser jerked in shock and amazement at seeing the two of us there. <What? The Andalite child and his pet? Still alive?>

<Yes, still alive,> I said.

The four Mortrons wheeled their way into the vortex and came panting beside the visser. The Yeerk looked around, as if searching for a weapon. He stared at the Time Matrix while keeping his stalk eyes on me.

"Elfangor," I heard Loren moan.

I swept one stalk eye toward her and almost cried out. Her hair was now so long that it piled on the ground. And her toenails extended nearly a foot through the fabric of her artificial hooves. Her hands were like hideous claws.

<Stand perfectly still,> I said. <Hold out your hands and don't move them.>

FWAPP! FWAPP! FWAPP! FWAPP!

With four quick tail swipes I cut most of the finger and toenail away. At the same time I kept my main eyes on the visser. He was watching me closely. Sizing me up.

<I suppose we'll have to agree to work together again,> he said.

<The same thing would happen,> I said. <Another compromised universe. No better than this one. Only this time we'd all be more careful to bring allies and weapons from our memory.>

The Yeerk visser shrugged. <At least then we'd have a fair fight.>

"He doesn't want to fight you one-on-one," Loren said.

<No, he'd rather have a host of allies and weapons,> I agreed.

But Loren shook her head, which caused a ripple through the massive pile of her golden hair. "No, it's more than that. He's afraid to fight you one-on-one. I saw it in his face."

The idea seemed ludicrous. Loren liked me and assumed I was the better fighter. But that was no way to judge. Visser Thirty-two had the body *and* mind of Alloran. All of Alloran's speed and experience.

"He *is* afraid, Elfangor," Loren insisted.

<Afraid of *what*?> the visser laughed. <Of this Andalite child? My Mortrons and I will annihilate him!>

"Really? So why not do it? Why talk about working together?" Loren turned to me. "Alloran has seen you tail fight, Elfangor. That knowledge is the visser's now, right? That's why he's scared."

The Yeerk stared hatred at Loren. <I'll be sure to kill you slowly, human.> He shot a glance at the four Mortrons. <Kill!> he yelled suddenly.

The Mortrons powered their wheels and came for us. The visser was right behind them.

It had come down to this. To a tail fight to the death between me and Visser Thirty-two. I tried to recall everything Old Sofor, my fighting trainer, had taught me. But I couldn't remember a thing.

The Mortrons launched their bird portions. Leather wings spread wide and vicious mouths wider still. I had to take them out of the fight without cutting them. If I cut them in pieces they would simply regenerate.

SWOOP!

FWAPP! I struck! But at the last second I turned my blade aside and hit the Mortron with the flat side of the blade.

THWACK! The bird portion went flying. It fell to the ground and didn't move. I had knocked it out.

Two bird portions went for Loren, jagged teeth glistening from their long mouths. She swung her softball bat but missed. The bat fell from her hands as a Mortron bird portion slapped her head with its wings.

One of the Mortrons was still after me, and as he swooped the visser attacked.

Mortron and Andalite tail struck at me.

<Aaarrrgghh!> The Mortron ripped a gash in the side of my head, barely missing my stalk eyes! My own blood spurted, and then the visser's tail was . . .

Blocked! FWAPP! I knocked his blow aside.

FWAPP! He struck again!

I dodged beneath the blow and fired my own tail, but my aim was thrown off by the Mortron, who twisted back and came at me again.

"No! No! No, you don't!" I heard Loren cry.

She was under attack from the other two Mortrons! I saw bright red human blood. But if I tried to help her, the visser would kill me before I could so much as twitch.

It was impossible!

FWAPP! The visser struck, and this time the blow hit home. I saw a line drawn through the skin of my chest. The line opened to become a gash.

FWAPP! He struck! I parried the blow, but barely.

<Ah, not so fast after all, are you, Andalite?> the visser crowed.

In seconds the fight would be over. I knew it. I had lost. Loren was probably already done for.

But then, through one twisted stalk eye, I saw Loren. To my astonishment she had her two strong human hands wrapped around the neck of one of the Mortron bird portions.

She was choking it! And the other Mortron was tangled in the wild mess of her hair.

<This fight isn't over yet, Visser!> I said, and I struck!

FWAPP!

He blocked my blow. I struck again!

FWAPP! A hit!

<Aaaahhhh!> the visser moaned in pain.

But my own Mortron hit me without warning. A painful slice of my right rear haunch.

Then I saw a frightening thing. Loren's strong human hands were choking the life from the Mortron bird portion. And her fingernails, growing so fast that I could actually see them grow, were growing *into* the Mortron.

FWAPP! The visser struck.

I parried and turned my parry into a thrust!

<Yes!> I exulted as my tail blade plunged deep into the visser's left arm.

But the remaining Mortron was coming back around, aiming straight for my face this time. With a sneer, the visser struck.

Mortron teeth and the Yeerk's stolen Andalite tail blade flew at me.

I could stop only one.

But whichever strike got through, bird or blade, would finish me.

chapter 12

The Mortron flew at me!

The visser's blade split the air, aiming at my head!

Something moving! To my left, not fast by Andalite standards, but fast enough.

Loren spun the dead Mortron in her hand around and threw it with all her might. The Mortron slipped off the end of Loren's claw fingernails. It flew through the air and hit the other Mortron head on.

"Softball!" Loren yelled.

The Mortron that had been attacking me was knocked down. I swept my tail blade right to left and knocked the visser's blade away. It came within a hair of my face.

Loren calmly picked up her softball bat from the spot where it had fallen. And she annihilated the last Mortron, the one that had been tangled in her hair.

I think it was that very moment when I decided I could definitely get to like humans. At first they seemed almost ridiculously weak, tottering around on their two legs, having to make sounds to communicate, lacking anything in the way of tail or other defenses.

But humans had some definite possibilities.

<Nice throw,> I said.

"It's called a pitch," Loren said. She smiled. "Thanks."

<Your Mortrons are done for, Visser,> I said to him. <It's just you and me now. Tail-to-tail.>

The Yeerk slug called Visser Thirty-two glared hatred at me through his stolen Andalite eyes. <You think you've won, Andalite? You think you can kill me now? Guess again. You haven't thought it through. But then again, I have the advantage of adding Alloran's Andalite knowledge to my own. What do you think will happen to whoever is left behind in this universe once it is broken apart?>

I had to struggle to think. An artificial universe . . . composed of the thoughts and memories of three different individuals . . .

<What? Over your head, is it? A collapsed time line returns us each to our own proper space-time location.>

<So you go back to the *Jahar*. Back to being sucked into a black hole. I can live with that, Yeerk. I don't care how you die. Here, from my tail.

Or there, drawn helplessly into a black hole. So long as you die. You are an abomination. The first Andalite-Controller. I just want you to be the last.>

"I told you he was scared to fight you," Loren said.

<I guess you were right.>

The visser hesitated. But I knew he would walk away. I could feel his resolve failing. But his malice, his evil remained as strong as ever.

<The day will come, Elfangor, when I will destroy you. I will make it personal. I will make it very personal.>

Then he turned and plunged back into the vortex wall.

"That's the end of him."

<No. I don't think so,> I said. I won't say I had a vision. I don't believe much in supernatural things. But I felt deep down that the visser and I would find our time lines entwined again someday.

"So now what? We have to get out of here fast. My hair is still growing. My nails are out of control. I feel like I'm getting older. My . . . well, I'm getting older, I'll leave it at that. But I swear I'm suddenly eighteen!"

<Yes. Your face is changing. And I, too, feel myself changing. We must leave. But this time there can only be one person directing the Time Matrix.

We have to go somewhere real. Somewhere that is a part of the true universe.>

"The Andalite world?"

<No,> I said heavily. <What would I do if I went back to my own people? I mutinied against Alloran, my prince. I left Arbron behind to live as a Taxxon. And I know too many secrets. I know that my own people did use a Quantum virus in the Hork-Bajir war. What might they do if they suddenly had the Time Matrix?>

"I guess sometimes even good people do bad things. I mean, that's what war is all about, isn't it?"

<If we use the Time Matrix to win this war we will no longer be Andalites. Not what I think of as Andalites, anyway. We have to win this war by being ourselves. By living up to our own standards, not by becoming as brutal and ruthless as the Yeerks are.>

"You mean what's the point of winning, if by winning you lose what you were fighting for."

<Yes. That's exactly what I mean. I can't give my people the Time Matrix. And I can't let the Yeerks have it, either. And it cannot be destroyed, only hidden.>

Loren looked strangely at me. "You're going to hide it on Earth?"

<Earth. Yes. And this time no nosy, greedy Skrit Na will stumble across it.>

"What do you want me to do?"

<Imagine your Earth, your home, just as it is today. Picture every last detail. Your mother. Your friends. Your hollow human house. Picture the time just after the Skrit Na took you. An hour afterward.>

"That was like, what, a week ago? Did all this happen in just a week?"

<Yes. Just a week. And we need to go back in time. Back before your mother would have noticed you missing. But not before the Skrit Na took you or we would undo this entire time line.>

"Maybe we *should* erase this time line. Save Arbron. Save Alloran."

<And the two of us never meet?>

"I wouldn't want that."

<Me neither. But more importantly, we wouldn't know the exact effects of rewriting all that history. It may mean the Skrit Na escaped clean with the Time Matrix and delivered it to the Yeerks. No. We have to keep our time line intact. And as long as the *you* you've been this last week doesn't encounter some second *you*, we'll be fine.>

"There's one more problem. This *me* has aged. I'm older. I must be almost eighteen now, judging from the way I've grown. People would notice."

<Yes. But imagine that they don't. Imagine that you are eighteen and that everyone who has ever known you expects you to be eighteen.>

"Is this really going to work?"

<I don't know, Loren. Nothing else I've tried has worked so far.>

She smiled with her human mouth. "Then I'll take care of driving the Time Matrix. Let's go."

She placed her hands against the Time Matrix and closed her eyes.

The swirl tightened around us, and I saw images flash by. Images of a planet I had never visited, but already knew and cared for.

And then we were a million light-years, and one week, away.

chapter 13

Three years later . . .

I ran away from the great war of Yeerk against Andalite.

I ran away and hid on the planet called Earth. I buried the Time Matrix in a patch of woods. I performed a *Frolis Maneuver*: the mixing of different DNA to form a single morph. I found ways to come in contact with humans and absorb bits of several DNA patterns. And when I had enough, I morphed a human for the first time.

And for the last time. You see, I was done with the fight. I had done all I could, and I had made a mess of things. My people would be better off without me. And there was no way to hide over the long term. I had to become a human. And stay a human.

I attended a human college. I majored in physics. It was hard. Hard to pretend not to know all the answers instantly. I had to pretend to struggle with equations I had known perfectly since childhood.

And it was hard being a human. I missed my stalk eyes. I missed my tail terribly. But I didn't want to fight anymore. I was done with the war. Sick to death of it.

Besides, there were good things about being a human. The human sense of taste is wonderful. Almost overpowering.

And then there was Loren. She had recreated her own life to deal with the fact that she had aged several years. She went back to a mother who never knew she had been gone. Back to friends and family who all expected her to be the age she now was.

The power of the Time Matrix is awesome. I had seen what it could do, and I was more convinced than ever that it could not be given to either side in a terrible, bloody war. Desperate people do desperate, evil things.

I finished college at an accelerated rate. Not surprising, since I was a century or two ahead of all the professors. I began graduate school. But I was bored there, too.

I had a job writing software for primitive human computers. It was the 1980s on Earth and humans were just beginning to understand computers.

I met a lot of humans who were working in the computer field. My human friend Bill used to come over to my room and we would exchange ideas. It was hard for me to simplify my knowledge enough for him to follow. Everything had to be explained in simple human terms, using words like "window" to explain a childishly simple concept.

And my human friend Steve thought it was a huge breakthrough to use symbolic icons and a simple pointer rather than a lot of complex language.

One day I got a terrible shock. I saw Chapman at the college. I was with Loren at the time. Chapman did not recognize her. He did not know her at all.

It made no sense. We had left Chapman back on the *Jahar*, tumbling toward a black hole. He should have been swallowed by the black hole, crushed and annihilated.

Loren tested him. She went up to him and said, "Hello, Chapman. Heard from your old friend Visser Thirty-two lately?"

He'd stared at her like she was confused. This Chapman recalled nothing. His memory had been erased.

I tried to put it out of my mind. I told myself Chapman had a twin, or that it was some unknown physics of black holes. But it nagged at me. From then on I felt a sense of being watched. And I wondered if, or when, the power that had rewritten Chapman's memory would make itself known.

But the most important thing I did as a human was to marry Loren.

We had come to care about each other on our adventure. And when she was ready by human standards, I married her.

And I really thought that I had left everything behind me. I thought that I was a human now. That Earth would be my home. That I would remain far, far away from the terrible space battles that raged across the galaxy, around stars so distant I could not even find them in Earth's night sky.

I left my own people. My own species. And I was human . . . except in the dreams where I would run across the open grass and speak to the trees and whip my tail around for the simple joy of it.

We got a house. What I used to call a hollow house. Now I understood human things.

I drove a car. A yellow Mustang like the one I'd driven on the Taxxon world. And I only thought of my own people, and my own family, and my own world some of the time. Not every minute.

Not *every* minute.

I even took a human name. Alan Fangor. It was Loren's idea. See, humans shorten their names, just as Andalites do. So most people called me Al Fangor.

One day I drove my car home from my job and parked it in the driveway. I could see that Loren was not home. Her own car was not in the driveway. She had gone to see a doctor. Although human doctors were practically barbarians who could not even eliminate a simple tumor without cutting holes in a person!

I stepped out of the car on my two human legs. It turned out, much to my surprise, that I seldom fell over, even with just two legs.

I walked up the driveway to the door and opened it, as I had done a thousand times before. Only this time someone was standing in my living room.

He was a man. A human. Or so I thought.

"What are you doing in here?" I demanded in angry mouth sounds.

The man looked at me with amusement. I was good at reading human expressions now. "What am I doing here? What are *you* doing here?"

"I live here. This is my home." I was a little fearful. Human arms are strong and can be used for fighting. But whenever I sensed danger, I missed my tail. And I felt vulnerable, being unable to see behind me.

The man shook his head sadly. "Elfangor-Sirinial-Shamtul, this is *not* your home."

My knees weakened and I almost collapsed. I made it to the couch and sat down heavily. "What are you?" I asked.

He laughed. "You don't ask *who* I am. You ask *what*. You are still wise enough to know I am not human."

"Just tell me what you want," I snapped.

"I don't want anything. *We* don't want anything. We do not interfere in the problems of other species."

"We? Who is we?"

"The 'we' whose machine you have used to alter the direction of time and space."

"Ellimist?" I whispered fearfully.

"Yes. I am one of those creatures you call Ellimists."

chapter 14

I couldn't believe it. I had never been sure I believed in Ellimists. I still wondered if it was some kind of trick. He looked fully human. But of course, for a true Ellimist, such things are easy.

"Am I really an Ellimist?" the man asked, mocking. "Let's see. I know that Arbron still lives in the tunnels of the Living Hive. I know that you made a universe once, you and the human and the Yeerk called Visser Three."

I jerked in surprise. "Visser *Three*?"

"Yes, he's advanced quite far in the Yeerk hierarchy."

"He should be dead!"

"*Should* be dead? Do you really think you can play games with time itself? Do you think you can change things around to suit you and not make a mess of it? Are you so naive, Andalite, that you can't understand that time is a trillion, trillion, trillion strands, all woven and interwoven? That if you twist and break one strand it may have unforeseen effects in a thousand other places and times?"

"He's alive. The visser."

"Yes. He is alive. He still inhabits Alloran's body." The Ellimist focused gray human-seeming eyes on me. "He is a terrible enemy of your people."

I shook my head. "Humans are my people now."

"Like the human named Chapman? Is he one of your people?

"You. It was you. You brought him back here and erased his memory."

"I undid an error in the time-space continuum. Chapman plays a part in what is still to come."

"I don't care," I said harshly. "I don't care about wars in far-off space."

"Far off? Do you really think you are safe here, Elfangor? Do you assume the Yeerks will never come?"

I felt my throat clutching up. It happens to humans when they are upset or afraid. "Will they come here?"

"Elfangor, the first Yeerk advance scouts are in orbit above Earth right now."

I said nothing for a long time. I looked out of the window, expecting to see Loren's car pull up at any moment. But then I realized what a fool I was being. If the Ellimist didn't want us to be interrupted, we wouldn't be.

"There's nothing I can do," I said at last. "I tried my hand at being a hero. I failed."

"Failed? You kept the Time Matrix from falling into the hands of either side, Yeerk or Andalite. You saved the galaxy."

"I couldn't save Arbron. I helped destroy Alloran and deliver him to the Yeerks to create the abomination he became. I wasn't able to destroy that abomination. I was weak. I was foolish."

"You refused to slaughter defenseless prisoners. You refused to destroy yourself in order to win a battle. You are wise, for a primitive creature. But you also altered the course of time by using the Time Matrix. And that has created awful problems. For your people. For *both* your peoples. Your peoples need you."

I laughed. "No one needs me."

"You are not *where* and *when* you should be, Elfangor."

"The galaxy will get along without me."

The Ellimist leaned forward and put his face close to mine. "No. It won't."

"What do you want from me?!" I yelled, suddenly enraged.

"We want nothing."

"Liar! Why are you here if you don't want anything?"

"We do not interfere in the affairs of other species."

"Then go away! Get out! Leave me alone!"

"We do not interfere. But sometimes we repair what has been shattered."

I froze. What stupid game was he playing? He wouldn't interfere, but he would? Which was it? What did he want?

"What do I want? Nothing. But I can tell you that you have twisted and distorted time. Things are not as they should be. Battles are lost that should have been won. What should be safe is now endangered."

"I can't go back," I pleaded. "I'm not an Andalite anymore. I'm human! I have a wife. I have a place here."

"All a product of your meddling," the Ellimist said. "The human girl Loren was meant to marry a human. You were meant to be a warrior. A great hero to your people. A mentor and guide to your brother."

"I have a brother? He was born? I knew my family was preparing —"

"In this broken time line, no. But you *should*. He has a job to do. And so does another person who you do not even know exists. Elfangor, without you, your people, both your peoples, will be slaves of the Yeerks."

I jumped back to my feet. "You're lying. Manipulating me. Using me."

"We don't use anyone. We don't interfere. But if you ask me to fix the mess you have made . . . to repair the time line so that you return to your destiny . . . that, and that alone, I can do."

I wanted to hit him. I wanted to throw up. I hated the galaxy and everything in it.

"There is a battle, Elfangor. A turning point. Visser Three is there. You are supposed to be there. Right now."

"I can't leave Loren."

"Listen to me, Elfangor. Visser Three will come to Earth one day. He remembers her. He remembers that she mocked him. Do you know what he will do to her? And will you be able to stop him, when he is surrounded by a thousand of his own troops?"

I felt warm liquid run down my cheeks. Tears. A human thing.

"And if I go back . . . if I ask you to repair the time line . . . will it save Earth? Will it save the Andalites? And my Loren?"

"No. Not by itself. But what is impossible now will become possible again."

I looked at the creature who posed as a human. The creature who had the power to make entire solar systems disappear. "What game are you playing, Ellimist?"

"Will you cross-examine me, Andalite? Or will you ask me to undo the mess you have made?"

"Loren . . . ?"

"Will never know you existed. But you will know. You will still have your memories."

I tried to smile, but it twisted cruelly on my lips. "You said something about a battle, Ellimist . . ."

"Come. I will carry you there. I will undo what was done, and repair the fabric of your fate, Elfangor."

chapter 15

Once, a long time before, I had explained to Loren what it must be like to see the universe as the Ellimists saw it. And now, as the Ellimist lifted me up out of the everyday world of three dimensions of space and one of time, I saw what he saw.

When I had used the Time Matrix I glimpsed the lines of time interwoven. But now I saw a thousand times more. It was beyond sight. Beyond sound. It was some new sense, some new awareness.

I could feel the lines of time flowing through me. I could see and taste and hear and touch and smell a billion possibilities, all flowing through me.

I saw the Ellimist himself, as he really was. An indescribable being of light and time and space. Huge, but without a place. Alone, but not the only one of his kind. I saw and understood the vast power that trailed the lines of time through his grasp. And yet, against the enormity of all that had ever been and all that would ever be, I saw his limits, too.

The Ellimist was mighty. But not all-powerful.

I saw a young Andalite who looked like I had once: so serious, so determined to prove himself. I heard his name in my mind: Aximili-Esgarrouth-Isthill.

Hello, little brother, I said silently.

I saw Arbron, still alive on the Taxxon world. I felt his Taxxon hunger. But I also felt his Andalite pride.

Hello, Arbron. You have become the hero I always wanted to be.

I saw Loren, and wrapped around her time line now was another human who would be her mate. I had been written out of her memory. It tore at my heart to realize that I was now a stranger to her.

And yet, I saw that some part of my own time line still intersected her own. I still touched her future in some way. My line and hers converged, and then from those two lines came a new line, just emerging, just beginning to grow.

<What does it mean?> I asked the Ellimist.

YOU HAVE A SON, ELFANGOR.

In a flash I saw the truth. That's why Loren had gone to see her doctor. She would have come home and told me. We had a child!

<No! You can't take me away! I have a son!> I cried. <That changes everything! Don't take me away!>

YOU *ARE* AWAY, ELFANGOR-SIRINIAL-SHAMTUL. WHAT WAS BROKEN HAS BEEN REPAIRED. YOU ARE WHERE YOU MUST BE. THE CHILD WILL BE RAISED AS THE SON OF AN-OTHER.

<But my son! What will happen to him? Will he still . . . exist?>

I saw the tiny line that was my son flow off through time. I saw pain and hardship and loneli-ness for him.

But then, like a distant nova, I saw a flash of light, far at the edge of a still-uncertain future. Across the galaxy my brother's line reached to join with my son's. And four other bright, shining time lines formed together with those two.

I knew I was watching something incredible and important. And I knew this union of six time lines, one Andalite and five human, was the entire point of the Ellimist's "noninterference."

<So, you don't interfere with the affairs of other species?> I asked him.

WAS THAT SARCASM, ELFANGOR? the Ellimist asked. And then he laughed a huge laugh that reverber-ated through all the tendrils of space and time.

<Is it all just a game for you?>

YES, the Ellimist said, all laughter silent now. BUT WE ARE NOT THE ONLY GREAT POWERS OF THE GALAXY. THERE IS ANOTHER. OLDER EVEN THAN WE. AND HE PLAYS A DARK GAME, ANDALITE. IT IS WITH HIM THAT WE PLAY. SO

HOPE THAT WE WIN, ELFANGOR-SIRINIAL-SHAMTUL. HOPE THAT WE WIN.

I saw a battle ahead.

I saw my own body twisting and changing shape.

I opened my stalk eyes. Tested my Andalite tail.

And all at once, I was on the bridge of an Andalite fighter.

chapter 16

I heard the chaotic thought-speak voices of crying, dying Andalites in my head.

<Main engines down, we have lost maneuvering power!>

<We're at dead stop!>

<Break off! Break off! He's on me!>

I looked down at my display. The *StarSword* lay helpless, unable to move. Yeerk Bug fighters swarmed around her, firing Dracon beams at maximum power.

The defenses were failing. As I watched, one of the Dome ship's engines was blown completely away from the ship. An explosion without sound in the vacuum of space.

The Yeerk pool ship sat like a fat spider gloating over its kill. The *StarSword* was finished. The Yeerks could finish her off at leisure.

But still the warriors aboard the Dome ship fought on. I heard their thought-speak cries to the few remaining Andalite fighters.

<Seerian, watch out! Bug fighter on your tail!>

<Separate the Dome! Give them two targets to deal with!>

And then, <To all fighters. This is the captain. We are beginning self-destruct sequence. Clear the area. If anyone is still alive out there, get clear of the *Star-Sword*. We will implode the engines and blow a hole in space. Maybe we can take some of those Bug fighters down with us. Self-destruct in three minutes,> he said heavily, and then added, <We have done our duty.>

Now there was a new ship on my viewscreen. All black. Shaped like some ancient battle-ax.

The Blade ship of a visser.

It swooped in close to the doomed, powerless *StarSword*. And with its Dracon beams it began to slice away the remaining two engines. The *Star-Sword* would not be allowed to self-destruct.

<Fighters! Any fighters, try to draw that Blade ship off!>

The captain's call went unanswered. There were no fighters left.

So this was the battle the Ellimist wanted me to join. This was where I was supposed to be. I called up ship-to-ship communications. <Hang on, *Star-Sword*. I'll take care of that Blade ship.>

<Who the . . . who is that?>

<Elfangor. I mean, *Aristh* Elfangor-Sirinial-Shamtul.>

<What by all the bloody tails of Crangar are *you* doing here?>

<It's a long story, Captain. I hope I'll have the chance to tell it to you.> I switched channels to broadcast in the open. On a frequency the Yeerks would monitor.

I aimed the fighter straight at the Blade ship. I punched up a nice, medium burn. And then I called up the Blade ship. <Andalite fighter calling the Yeerk visser.>

A Hork-Bajir face appeared on the monitor. "Who are you to call upon the visser? If you are pleading for mercy, I can laugh at you as well as he!"

<Pleading for mercy? Not likely. Tell the visser that an old friend is here to see him. Tell him that Elfangor has come to finish what we began in a vortex, a long time ago.>

In a flash the screen image changed. And there was the Andalite face that had once belonged to War-prince Alloran.

<You!> he cried.

<I have to congratulate you on escaping from that black hole. And I hear you've been promoted, Yeerk. Visser *Three*. Very impressive. But I have to tell you, Yeerk, I am aimed straight for your ship. And in exactly ten seconds I will punch up Maxi-

mum Burn. At this distance it will take me less than two seconds to impact your ship.>

<You're bluffing!>

<Ten . . . Nine . . .>

<You'd be killed as well as me.>

<Yes. I would. Seven . . . Six . . .>

<All Dracon beams on that fighter!> Visser Three shouted to his crew.

The Blade ship turned to bring its Dracon beams forward where they could be aimed at me.

<You don't have enough time, Visser,> I said. <And once I punch a Maximum Burn it'll be too late. Four . . . Three . . .>

His main eyes blazed hatred at me.

<Two . . . One . . .>

<Get us out of here, top speed!> Visser Three screamed at his helmsman.

The Blade ship's engines glowed bright and the ship broke away from the *StarSword*.

<You think you've won, Andalite?> Visser Three sneered. <You're still just one fighter. And your Dome ship is crippled. I'll swing around, move off, and finish you in my own good time.>

<I wouldn't swing around just yet, Visser. See, you've cost me too much. And I am going to put an end to you right now. Computer? *Maximum Burn!*>

FWOOOOOOSH!

My engines lit up and I was blown back across the fighter's cramped bridge.

BOOOOOOM!

My fighter hit the neck of the Blade ship, slicing the diamond-shaped bridge away from the rest of the ship.

But I didn't see that. The impact knocked me out and tore both the fighters' engines and its shredder completely off.

I should have died.

But I didn't.

Minutes after I crippled the Blade ship, the Andalite Dome ship *TailStrike* came out of Zero-space less than a light year away. The Yeerks decided it was time to leave. Their Pool ship put a containment field around the parts of the broken Blade ship and made for Zero-space.

When I woke up, back aboard the *StarSword*, I was already a hero. The lost *aristh* who had returned mysteriously, years after disappearing, and had flown his fighter in a bold suicide mission.

I had saved the *StarSword*. I was made a full warrior. The captain himself told me that I would be a prince within a couple of years.

I had plenty of time, while recovering from my injuries, to figure out what to tell the captain. I considered all sorts of lies. But in the end, I told him everything. I wanted someone to know, now that Loren no longer did.

I told the captain everything . . . except for the location of the Time Matrix.

When I was done he looked at me for a long time in silence. At last he said, <You realize, Elfangor, that this story will never become public. You are a great hero, and our people need heroes. The details of your story would just confuse the issue.>

<But, Captain, I committed mutiny against War-prince Alloran. I failed to save Arbron. And . . . and in the end, I ran away.>

He looked at me very seriously. <Young warrior, do you think I don't know what happened to Alloran? Do you think I don't know about the Quantum virus he unleashed in the battle for the Hork-Bajir world? Alloran was my friend. When we were young *arisths* together he was a gentle, decent youngster. And funny! He loved to joke and play tricks.>

<Alloran?> I blurted without thinking.

<Yes. Alloran. But war does terrible things to people. Some it raises to greatness. Others it destroys. You did not mutiny against Alloran. You defended the beliefs he used to hold dear. You stood up for the people.>

It was strange. I felt like crying. But I no longer had human eyes. So I cried the way an Andalite does. Inside. In my hearts.

<As for running away to this Earth place . . . no one can be brave every minute of every day. No one can be brave all the time. And now you have a second chance. We need warriors like you, Elfangor. Warriors who will not forget *why* they are fighting. Will you stand by the people in this awful time? Will you fight? Will you be their hero?>

I guess his words should have made me feel good. I had wanted once to be a hero. But now I saw what it meant. I could imagine the price I would have to pay. The things I might have to do. I could feel the weight of it settling down on me like a thousand pound stone.

<Yes, Captain,> I said. <I will fight.>

chapter 17

It was many years before I saw Earth again. I had fought more battles than I could count. I had won, and I had lost.

The war with the Yeerks dragged on and on. Neither side seemed able to destroy the other. I wondered sometimes if that was just the way it had to be, or if the Ellimists and their unnamed opponents were interfering to keep the war going forever.

Who knows?

A Zero-space rift had opened up between planet Earth and the busy centers of the galaxy. That happens sometimes. It meant that Earth, rather than being days away, was now months and months away.

Maybe it was coincidence. Or maybe it was those great powers of the galaxy, playing their games with the threads of space and time.

But finally we did return. We went to Earth because we got evidence of what I already knew: The Yeerks had targeted Earth.

We went in the brilliant, brand-new Dome ship *GalaxyTree*. We came out of Zero-space and found ourselves outnumbered. We fought, but this time there was no last-minute rescue.

The Dome was separated from the ship and plunged into Earth's sea. My brother, Aximili, a young *aristh* as I had been, was aboard.

And I, desperate enough to break my own vow, took my damaged fighter down to the planet, looking for the place where I had long ago hidden the Time Matrix.

By the time I landed I was too weak from my injuries to even think about finding the Time Matrix. It was buried beneath the concrete foundation of a half-finished building. What had once been peaceful forest was now a construction site.

I lay there dying, knowing that Visser Three would pursue me. Knowing that this time, at long last, he would win over me.

And that's when five human children, no older than Loren had been when I first met her, came by. Three boys and two girls. Scared at the sight of me. But not so scared that they ran away.

One of them seemed especially drawn to me. And when I saw his face, I knew why.

He could only be Loren's son. *My* son.

"Hello," the one called Tobias said to me.

I broke our Andalite law and gave these children the power to morph. See, I knew what human children can do.

The Yeerks came and I told the human children to hide. But Tobias stayed behind with me for just a few moments. Alone.

<Your mother . . . tell me about your mother, Tobias. Your family.>

He was surprised. Troubled. "She . . . disappeared. When I was just little. I don't know what happened. I guess she died. People say she just left because she was messed up. They said she never got over my father. I don't know. But I know she has to be dead because she'd never have just left me. No matter what. But maybe that's just what I told myself. I don't exactly have a family."

It was a fresh stab of pain in my hearts. And yet, I knew now that all was not lost.

<Go to your friends, Tobias. They are your family now.>

That's when I knew there was still hope for my adopted people, the humans of Earth. My son had survived. He was strong in ways even he did not suspect. He would change the course of history.

And oh, as I lie here now, seconds from death, clutched in the power of Visser Three's monstrous morph, I can see clearly what I only guessed at before.

I remember seeing the time line that curled away from Loren and me. And I remember the burst of light as it was joined with four other human lines, and the line of my own little brother.

Tobias was that line. And joined with these others, he held powers that would make Visser Three tremble.

I, Elfangor-Sirinial-Shamtul, having transmitted all my last thoughts and memories to be sent through space to my people, now end my life.

My *hirac delest* is done. I go in peace to my death. And I leave as my last legacy a single word for all the free peoples of the galaxy.

<Hope . . .>